LUMI
THE STORY OF A LITTLE LIGHT FAIRY

BY
Pete Martin

With thanks to my wife Phil and my sister Karen for their on-going support and advice.

With BIG thanks also to Elle and Jack, who just like Lumi, brought light into our lives during dark and uncertain times. May you continue to share your happiness, love and joy with us all.

Lumi, The Story Of A Little light Fairy: ©Pete Martin 2021.
First Edition: ©Pete Martin 2021.
Editor: Pete Martin & Beatles Liverpool and More Ltd.
Cover Design: ©Pete Martin & Beatles Liverpool and More Ltd
Illustrator: ©Pete Martin
ISBN: 978-1-8381238-2-6

Come gather and listen all you young folk and old To the strangest story that's ever been told. The tale of a fairy - could it be a fairy tale? A story of courage, of trust and betrayal.

Enjoy as the story unfolds over time. And it's easy to follow as it's all told in rhyme.

Now this story began a long time ago.
In a strange little village called Cum-an-Go.

It's a good day's journey from Old London Town. With villagers inclined to WHIZZING around.

On their horses and carts through the village they flew. On ponies and traps and carriages too.

The roads of the village were packed don't you know. With the speed loving villagers reluctant to slow.

They all had bells fitted and rang them with glee. Convinced this would keep the roads up ahead free.

But the small village roads were too narrow for sure. And where the roads crossed there were crashes galore.

There were smashes and bashes with many folk hurt. The police and the Mayor were both put on alert.

"This daily disaster must stop!" the Mayor said. "Control of the traffic's the best way ahead!"

Now the Mayor – a cunning and nasty man too. Was hatching a plan which only he knew.

It involved a strange fellow from the village he'd seen. Who looked like a fairy and dressed all in green.

He'd seen this small neighbour perform such a sight. By smiling he'd turned his head into a light !

This fairy had powers that Mayor wanted to use. And he'd make him an offer that he couldn't refuse!

For he was smaller than anyone else round about. And Mayor's plan became clearer as he worked it all out.

'There were smashes and bashes with many folk hurt.'

"We could use this strange fellow!" Mayor grinned to himself. "To make our roads safe and improve village health."

Now the fairy called Lumi was small, brave and true. Guiding others through woodlands and forests he knew.

He was born without wings or a talent for flight. But was blessed with the gift of power over light.

Lumi's wife was a beautiful Lullaby Fairy. Who sang to calm little ones from things that were scary!

With their children they lived in a small mushroom home. Which Lumi had constructed all on his own.

They were happy but fearful of Goblins who tried. To scare Lumi's family and force them to hide.

You see Goblins are nasty and angry and scary. And knew Lumi's home was close to the dairy.

They hated all fairies and Elf folk as well. And were forcing them back to the Great Fairy Dell.

And though Lumi wasn't a fairy who fought. He could rattle those Goblins and had never been caught.

Each day he would guard his home and his kin. Keeping eyes wide open for sneaky Goblin.

Now Mayor called for Lumi to come straight away. To hear of his plan and the part Lumi'd play.

Mayor then told Lumi of the idea he had. To stop all the crashes so harmful and bad.

At the side of the crossroads a tall pole would stand. With a box made of green glass the size of a hand.

'Lumi could rattle those Goblins and had never been caught.'

Another beside it of red glass they'd fit. And Lumi between them would carefully sit.

When the main road was busy he would light up the red. Telling all other traffic to stop up ahead.

And when it was clear then the green light he'd show. To tell other traffic it was all safe to go.

And not a candle was needed to make the glass bright. Lumi's head could be used to make green or red light !

Now Lumi, who was caring, kind and courageous. Listened carefully to the Mayor for what seemed like ages.

And then he considered all the Mayor said. And knew that because of his size and his head.

It was Lumi alone who could take on the Mayor's task. But there was one burning question he just had to ask.

Who would keep the Goblins from his family so dear? "We will!" said the Mayor, "You'll have nothing to fear!

There'll be a policeman at your house every day. And unwanted visitors he'll send on their way."

Then the Mayor told Lumi he'd be a hero to all. There was no other villager so clever or small.

Who could take on this job which was special and tough. They would never be able to thank him enough!

And his family could safely visit as well. With safety precautions in case Lumi fell!

"A strong safety chain would be tied 'round your waist." Mayor sniggered and then he turned round in haste.

'Lumi's head could be used to make green or red light!'

So Lumi could not see the look the Mayor had. The look of a person who was scheming and bad.

So smiling and glowing Lumi took on the role. And the very next morning watched them put up the pole.

It didn't take long before he started his glowing. And green and red lights from the pole top were showing.

People waved as they safely passed by him each day. Some thanked him - some waved and some shouted hooray!

One morning an advisor to Her Majesty the Queen. Looked up to the light where Lumi was seen.

He waved at the fairy - who smiled and waved back. "What a marvellous way to keep us all safe on track!

I must tell the Queen," the advisor he thought. As his carriage took him back to Her Majesty's Court.

It wasn't too long before a motor- car was seen.
A horseless carriage! - painted black, gold and green.

Now months had gone by without one crash occurring. Lumi was a hero - but his sore head was whirring.

From all of the glowing he was having to do. But the villagers were grateful and much safer too.

Many were sad to see him tied to the light. With his little head glowing each day and each night.

And he couldn't get down - to hug his children or wife! Some thought he'd be up there for the rest of his life?

Then some weeks later when no family appeared. Lumi called for the Mayor – for he thought that was weird.

'It wasn't too long before a motor-car was seen. A horseless
carriage! painted black, gold and green.'

He asked for Mayor's help to make sure they were good. And a messenger went 'round as soon as he could.

But Lumi's family were gone! - There was no sign at all! When he shouted their names no one answered his call.

This news was then passed straight back to the Mayor. "Lumi's cottage was empty – there's nobody there!"

But the Mayor LIED to Lumi and said "They're all well - Just tired as far as the messenger could tell,

But they'd soon again visit the base of the pole" Relieved by these words Lumi stuck to his role.

He was happy that the villagers were now safe from harm. Without knowing that his family had to flee in alarm.

From a small Goblin crew who had turned up one day.
And forced his poor family to all run away!

They escaped to the woods and were desperate and gloomy. They were frightened and needed their brave Little Lumi.

They hoped that he'd come to find them real quick. As they hid in a den under shrubs that were thick.

And Lumi went on with his night and day glowing. But fear for his family inside him was growing,

For he still hadn't seen them at the pole any day. He was worried - despite what the Mayor had to say.

Then a day or so later with no traffic in sight. The Mayor and some workmen appeared by the light.

For the Mayor had been asked if he wanted to be. The first village in the land with electricity!

'They escaped to the woods and were desperate and gloomy.'

They'd illuminate Mayor's Hall and a street light or two. Cum-an-Go would be famous for sure the Mayor knew.

He agreed and then asked for one extra light. To stand by the crossroads if that was alright.

You see Lumi was becoming trouble for the Mayor. And it was time Mayor thought that he was no longer there!

They'd have the first Electric Traffic Light Control. And Mayor wanted the glory and fame for his role.

In making it happen and saving lives too. With no mention of what Lumi had been forced to do.

So the Mayor unchained Lumi who slipped down the pole. Pleased something else would now take on his role.

This meant he could go to his cottage at last. But when he arrived - he was stunned and aghast!

No policeman in sight - and no family as well ! Something was wrong - he could easily tell.

The cottage was damaged and Lumi - he knew. That it must be the work of a bad Goblin crew.

Lumi ran to the Mayor to ask for his aid. And asked why a policeman had not stopped the raid.

And why Mayor had told him his family were fine. When clearly they'd all been gone for some time!

But the Mayor was too busy to talk or explain. The traffic light system had just started again.

He had to make sure it was working just fine. And then take out important visitors to dine.

'Lumi ran to the Mayor to ask for his aid.'

Lumi would have to return some time later. The Mayor had to attend to things far greater!

At hearing these words Lumi left in disgust. He thought that the Mayor was a man he could trust,

But he couldn't care less where his family might be. Or help Lumi bring them all back safely.

It would be up to Lumi - with some villagers too. Who were glad to help out – it's the least they could do.

They started by searching in all nearby places. Hoping to pick up some clues and some traces.

Of where his wife and two children might be. Would Goblins still be looking to capture all three!

Lumi hoped they would find a safe place to stay. And his search carried on as the day ebbed away.

Although he was sad Lumi forced out a smile. And with his head glowing - searching went on a while.

And just as tired villagers were about to go home. A tall thin stranger appeared - on his own.

Dressed in a suit with a top hat as well. "He's not here to help us," Lumi could tell.

The stranger was looking for the 'Traffic Light Fairy'. And was told in the village to look by the dairy.

He had an important message from the Queen. For an advisor had told her just what he had seen.

When Lumi had control of a traffic light system. Would he share with the Queen his knowledge and wisdom?

'The stranger was looking for the Traffic Light Fairy.'

And could he come and talk to the Queen straight away? But Lumi explained what had happened that day!

The man said he was sorry to hear of his plight. And he hoped Lumi's family would all be alright.

He said he'd return the very next day. And would help with the searching - if still underway.

Lumi thanked him and while the others went home. He continued to search in the woods all alone.

Looking for places a fairy might hide. Then suddenly Lumi's eyes opened wide!

There – under some bushes and shrubs don't you know. Lumi could make out a tiny, faint glow.

Moving slowly and carefully towards the dim light. He pulled back a bush and oh what a sight!

Straight up from the ground - a Goblin jumped out ! Lumi was shocked and let out a shout!

But before he could turn to run off and leave. The Goblin grabbed hold of his long tunic sleeve.

It must have been hiding until it was dark. That horrible creature with teeth like a shark.

This was the closest to a Goblin he'd been. Lumi twisted then dived down a hole he had seen.

The Goblin couldn't follow him under the ground. Into the tunnels that Lumi had found.

The little light fairy was as quick as a fly. Moving through tunnels that were hidden and dry.

'The Goblin grabbed hold of his long tunic sleeve.'

At last when he thought he was all safe and sound. He made his way up from deep underground.

When close to the surface and about to hop out. Lumi stopped as he heard a familiar shout.

"Lumi is that you?" his wife said, "We're here? We've been hiding for so long - we're frozen with fear!"

Lumi started to smile and his glow filled the air. As he looked to a corner and all huddled there.

Was his family all looking so cold and so scared. Rubbing tears from his eyes Lumi squinted and stared.

His loved ones were safe and he'd found them- all three! They must return to the cottage and back to safety.

He hugged them and told them to follow him out. Making sure that there weren't any Goblins about.

Staying close and all moving swiftly along. By sun-up they were back where they all belonged.

With his family all safely tucked up in bed. Lumi sat a-watching and resting his head.

But just as he did a knocking he caught. "It must be the villagers to help him," he thought.

But there all alone as he opened the door. Was the tall man he'd seen just one day before.

Who asked, "Are your family now safely with you?" Lumi whispered, "They're asleep after all they've been through."

"Wonderful!" the tall stranger replied with a smile. "Do you think I may talk with you just for a while?

'By sun-up they were back where they all belonged.'

I've a message form Her Majesty the Queen don't you see. She'd like you to come back to the palace with me."

Lumi told him that he couldn't leave his family again. After all their distress and their fear and their pain.

Then the tall man replied, "The Queen asked me to tell. That your family are invited to the palace as well!"

At this Lumi's face - it started to glow. He told the tall stranger they'd all love to go.

And asked could he wait 'till his loved ones awoke. And when they were up - with Lumi they spoke.

They all wanted to visit the palace of course. And to travel in a carriage that was pulled by a horse!

Soon all of the family were well on their way. And arrived at the palace much later that day.

Now during the journey the tall man told Lumi. That the queen was distressed and worried and gloomy,

For the traffic on the roads outside the Queen's home. Had got faster and the number of vehicles had grown.

Her carriage had been banged and bumped about too. And each day with more crashes – her drivers all knew,

One day it could be the Queen who is hurt! They needed a system to give traffic alerts.

"You see her carriage goes out every day without fail. Through sunshine or snow through showers or hail.

It takes the Queen out on her daily royal tour. With food and comfort for the sick and the poor.

'They all wanted to visit the palace of course. And travel in a carriage that was pulled by a horse.'

Now the Queen she had heard that in Cum-an-Go. A system of lights made traffic stop and go.

And no further accidents had taken place there. Could this be a system the palace could share?

And Her Majesty would like to see you my dear. She hopes you can help keep our busy roads clear.

Her carriage leaves daily and comes back much later. Do you think you could help make her royal visits safer?"

Lumi said "Can I think on it - tomorrow I'll tell" **Meanwhile in Cum-an-Go - all wasn't so well!**

The 'Lectric was broken and the traffic lights too. The Mayor needed Lumi to help them get through.

He summoned his helper and told him to run. To Lumi's small cottage and tell him to come,

As he must return quickly to his traffic light pole. And once again take on the traffic control!

When the helper returned to say Lumi was gone. The Mayor tried to find out and asked everyone,

If they knew where the family had disappeared to. At last he found out that one villager knew.

She told him that in the Queen's carriage they'd been. The Mayor was amazed saying – "What could that mean?"

He sent his helper to London by pony and trap. To find Lumi and family and bring them all back.

The Mayor shouted out – "Don't let him say no! We must have him back here in Cum-an-Go!"

'The 'lectric was broken and the traffic lights too!'

The helper set off - trotting quickly away. But wouldn't get to the palace until the next day.

Next morn as the Queen's carriage left the main gate. The Mayor's helper was still travelling – he mustn't be late!

And Lumi watched from a palace window to see. Just how dangerous and heavy the traffic could be.

From the window he could easily see all the roads. And all of the traffic – and wow! There was loads!

Then he saw in the distance a black cart and horse. Heading that way on a co-llision course!

It would hit the Queen's carriage and people as well! It was moving too fast as far as Lumi could tell.

And he could see the Queen's carriage just couldn't go down. Any other road he could see in the town.

"Stop that cart!" came a shout amidst the commotion. Lumi nodded his head - for he shared the same notion.

He must stop cart and horse - but needed some glass. It must be red and he must move fast.

With no glass in sight he grabbed cloth that was red. And tying it around the top of his head,

He leapt from the window and ran fast and straight. Down the main road near the large palace gate.

He sprinted along and as he ran he smiled. Noticing the horse coming at him looked wild.

He could hear hooves clatter and carriage wheels creak.' The royal carriage window opened and the Queen took a peek.

'Then he saw in the distance a black cart and horse. Heading that way on a co-llision course.'

She saw a small figure running - his head glowing red. She looked on in horror as he ran on ahead,

Straight into the path of the cart and its horse. Which was hurtling along with incredible force.

Towards the small figure and Queen's carriage too! But the driver was dozing! – what could anyone do?

Then hearing some shouts, a scream and a yell. He awoke – grabbed the reins and tried braking as well.

But as the cart got closer - everyone could see. It would crush the small figure as flat as could be!

But Lumi ran on without fear for his fate. Then the driver saw the red light- but was it too late?

People gasped as fairy met horse and trap. And clouds of dust rose with a snapping of straps!

The Queen couldn't look – "Was the little man dead?" "That little guy's had it!" a grumpy voice said.

Some folk were crying "What a brave little man - He would never have made it – we could tell as he ran."

"The driver of the pony-trap saw him too late." "That hero saved the Queen our dear Head of State!"

"The Queen would've kopped it if not for that man. Her carriage would be squashed like a broken tin-can."

"That brave little man – make sure he is found," The Queen said tearfully – "Please search the ground."

'People gasped as fairy met horse and trap. And clouds of dust
rose with a snapping of straps.'

"For his courage I must tell his family about. As I'm sure they'll now have to all live without.

Their brave and selfless little man -
His final act we'll have painted as soon as we can."

As beside the Queen - townsfolk carefully searched. Carts and carriages trundled and lurched.

Away from the scene that was sombre and calm. Except for the Mayor's helper who had damaged his arm.

While trying to control his spooked-out horse. Still jumping and kicking with unusual force.

Then somebody noticed that under the mare. Something was caught-up that shouldn't be there.

The driver bent down and sure enough spied. A little red object which he carefully untied.

And there to everyone's shock and dismay. Across the driver's hands the little man lay!

The driver said, "This must be the fairy I'm after. Oh I wish I had seen him a little bit faster!

Can anyone help him - I don't think he's dead?" He whispered as he took the cloth from Lumi's head.

"Send for my doctor!" the Queen shouted out. "He'll be in the palace somewhere about."

Soon the doctor came running with Lumi's poor wife. The Queen said, "Now hurry – you must save his life!"

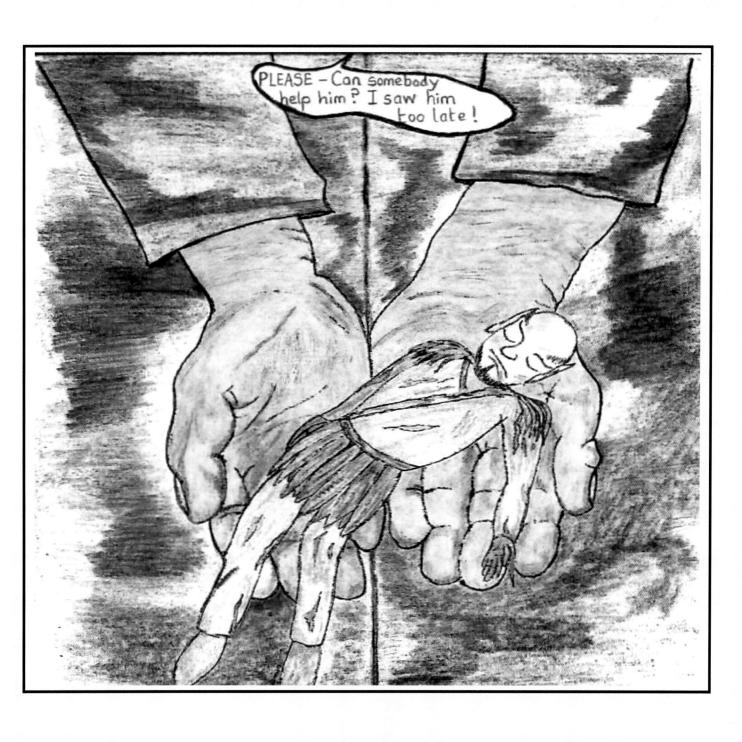

'And there to everyone's shock and dismay. Across the driver's hands the little man lay.'

Lumi lay - and the doctor tried all that he could. While Lumi's wife held his hand and sang as she would.

To make someone happy or feel at their ease. And suddenly Lumi spluttered and sneezed !

He opened an eye and saw a sweet-face so dear. Frowns turned to smiles and the Queen gave a cheer!

"You must be Lumi - pleased to meet you I'm sure. You just saved my life - you're a hero and more –

You're a shining example - brave, selfless and good. I hope you'll stay with us if you possibly could?"

Lumi sat up with his beautiful wife by his side. Both nodding and smiling – their joy not to hide.

Then the Mayor's helper heaved a sigh of relief. And gave Lumi his message - but kept it quite brief.

Lumi asked him to pass on his thanks to the Mayor. But tell him that his offer just doesn't compare.

To the job he'd been offered by Her Majesty the Queen. And his family was now safer than they'd ever been.

So to Cum-an-Go villagers and the Mayor too. Lumi sent his best wishes in all that they do.

**"And that's how Little Lumi saved the Queen from disaster
And why he'll live in the palace "Happily - Ever After!"**

'Lumi sat up with his beautiful wife by his side. Both nodding and smiling – their joy not to hide.'

LUMI
THE STORY OF A
LITTLE LIGHT FAIRY

THE END...
OR MAYBE NOT?

Perhaps Lumi might be called to help if the traffic lights near you go out!

The Beetle Who Loved To Sing.

This is a wonderful 26 page paperback book that all children will enjoy.

Size 210mm x 210mm

Ron the Beetle from Liverpool loves to sing and play the guitar. Along with his friends, Small George and Dingo, they form a band and attempt to take the world by storm!
In this charming children's poetry book, the author re-imagines the stories of the band conquering America in his own quirky way, set in the insect kingdom.

The Little Worm Who Lost His Wriggle.

This is a wonderful 32 page paperback book that all children will enjoy.

Size 210mm x 210mm

This is a beautifully illustrated rhyming story about a little worm who loses wriggle and because of this is unable to make his way home. With a little help from his friends: a Ladybird, a Frog, a Butterfly, a Snake and a young boy he finds his wriggle, and is reunited with his family.